RUFUS
and the
BLACKBERRY MONSTER

To my dad

Designed by Judith Robertson
Printed and bound in Belgium by Proost
for the publishers Piccadilly Press Ltd.,
5 Castle Road, London NW1 8PR

ISBN: 1 85340 593 0 (hardback)
1 85340 588 4 (paperback)

1 3 5 7 9 10 8 6 4 2

Set in Hiroshige Medium 18 pt

A catalogue record of this book is available from the British Library

Lisa Stubbs lives in Wakefield. She trained in Graphic Communications at Batley Art College and has illustrated greetings cards for a number of years. She has written and illustrated several successful books, also available from Piccadilly Press:

SONNY'S WONDERFUL
WELLIES
ISBN: 1 85340 495 0 (p/b)
1 85340 369 5 (h/b)
1 85340 551 5
(big book)

SONNY'S BIRTHDAY PRIZE
ISBN: 1 85340 427 6 (p/b)
1 85340 422 5 (h/b)

SONNY'S TREASURE HUNT
ISBN: 1 85340 571 X (p/b)
1 85340 555 8 (h/b)

ED AND MR ELEPHANT:
THE BIG SURPRISE
ISBN: 1 85340 565 5 (p/b)
1 85340 530 2 (h/b)

RUFUS
and the
BLACKBERRY MONSTER

Lisa Stubbs

Piccadilly Press • London

"Rufus and Archie," said Mrs Fox,
"I'm going to bake a pie for Amber's birthday tea.
I need you to pick some blackberries.
Off you go!"

Rufus loved blackberry pie, but he didn't like
the blackberry bush at the bottom of the garden.
It was BIG and DARK and SCARY!
"Be brave, Rufus," said Mrs Fox.
"Fill your bucket right up to the brim!"

As they walked down the garden path, Archie teased Rufus.

"The Blackberry Monster is hiding in the bush!"

"The Blackberry Monster!" said Rufus. His teeth began to chatter. "Who's the Blackberry Monster? He sounds very s-s-scary."

"He is," grinned Archie. "He's purple
and he has BIG ears, a BIG nose,
LONG whiskers and a LONG tail!
If he catches us he'll eat us up in ONE GULP!"
Archie giggled as Rufus shivered all over.

The blackberry bush loomed up ahead of them.

"You start here," said Archie in a bossy voice.

"I'll pick on the other side."

He sniggered as he disappeared.

He had taken the sunny side for himself.

Rufus was left alone in the darkest part
of the bush.

"I MUST be brave,"
thought Rufus.

He picked the blackberries
faster and faster.

Ping! Ping! Ping!
They flew into his bucket.

Rustle, crackle, rustle, snap! went a noise.
Rufus turned around. There was nothing there.

Rustle, rustle, crackle, snap!
Rufus's ears pricked up with fright.
"Archie, is that you?" he called. There was no
answer. Rufus *knew* it was the Blackberry Monster.
Maybe he should just run back home,
and forget about being brave!

Rustle, crackle, rustle, snap!
The monster was getting closer.
Rufus saw a dark shadow with BIG ears, a BIG nose,
LONG whiskers and a LONG tail . . .

Suddenly Archie rushed out from behind the bush.

He wasn't laughing any more.

"It's the Blackberry Monster!" he yelled.

"It's coming to eat us up!"

Archie was so scared he tried to hide behind Rufus.
But Rufus remembered to be brave –
brave enough for both of them!
The shadow was getting BIGGER and BIGGER
and CLOSER and CLOSER . . .

Rufus took a deep breath and shouted,
"I'm not scared of you!"
"Eeeeek!" cried the Blackberry Monster.
There in front of Rufus was a little, tiny, squeaky . . .

. . . mouse!

Rufus started to giggle. "It's all right, Archie, you can look now. I've caught the Blackberry Monster!"
"Monster?" squeaked the mouse. "I'm not a monster.
I thought YOU were monsters!
I was so scared I dropped all my blackberries.
I haven't anything for my supper now."

"Then you'd better come home with us to
Amber's birthday tea. There'll be plenty to eat,"
said Rufus. He smiled at Archie.
Archie did his best to smile back.

Mrs Fox made the most extra delicious blackberry pie
for Amber's birthday tea. Rufus, Archie, Amber
and the tiny mouse ate it up in seconds.
Then Rufus told everyone about the Blackberry
Monster, and how brave he had been.
"I know who the Blackberry Monster is,"
said Mrs Fox, as she looked at their faces . . .

"You're ALL Blackberry Monsters!"